MOUNTAIN VIEW ELEMENTARY
12401 PERRY STREET
BROOMFIELD, COLORADO 80020

# Twenty Is Too Many

# • Kate Duke •

DUTTON CHILDREN'S BOOKS • NEW YORK

CIP Data is available.

Published in the United States 2000 by Dutton Children's Books,
a division of Penguin Putnam Books for Young Readers
345 Hudson Street, New York, New York 10014
http://www.penguinputnam.com/yreaders/index.htm
Designed by Amy Berniker
Printed in Hong Kong    First Edition
1 3 5 7 9 10 8 6 4 2
ISBN 0-525-42026-6

The artwork was rendered in acrylic, watercolor, pencil,
colored pencil, and colored inks.

**To Sidney**

**T**wenty guinea pigs can be too many.

Twenty guinea pigs can start to sink.

But twenty sinking guinea pigs

**minus ten diving guinea pigs**

**leaves ten**

floating guinea pigs.

$20-10=10$

# Ten floating guinea pigs

**minus one ballooning guinea pig**

leaves nine

**waving guinea pigs.**

10-1=9

# Nine waving guinea pigs

# minus one swinging guinea pig

leaves eight

**seasick guinea pigs.**

9-1=8

Eight seasick guinea pigs

**minus one exploring guinea pig**

leaves seven

**excited guinea pigs.**

8-1=7

**Seven excited guinea pigs**

**minus one sneaky guinea pig**

leaves six

**yelling guinea pigs.**

7-1=6

**Six yelling guinea pigs**

**minus one fishing guinea pig**

leaves five

**flabbergasted guinea pigs.**

6-1=5

Five flabbergasted guinea pigs

**minus one surfing guinea pig**

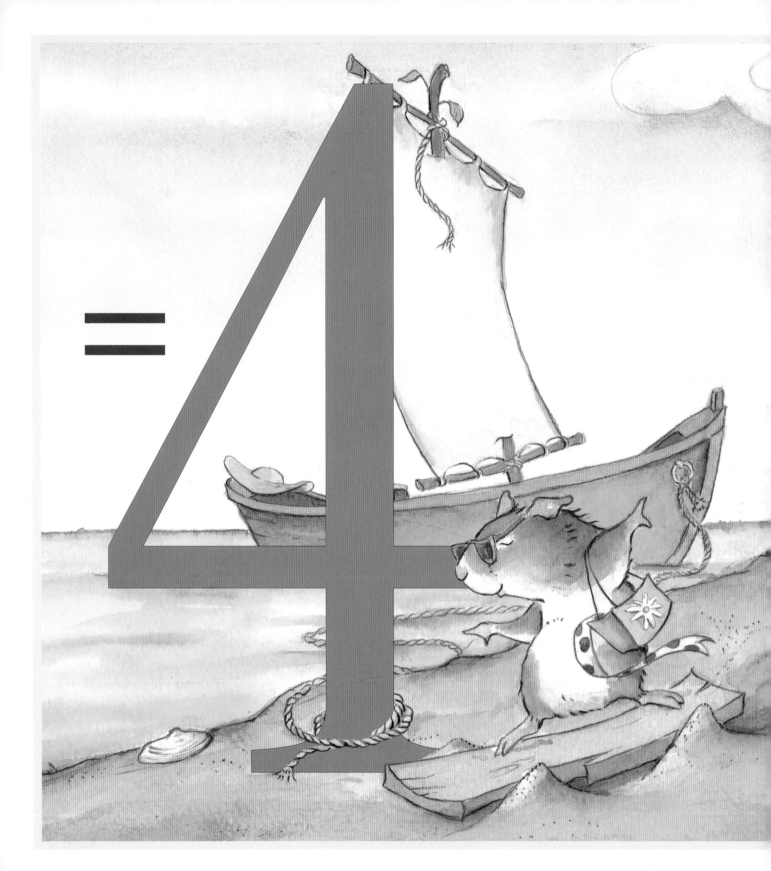

leaves four

**copycatting guinea pigs.**

5-1=4

Four copycatting guinea pigs

**minus one belly-flopping guinea pig**

leaves three

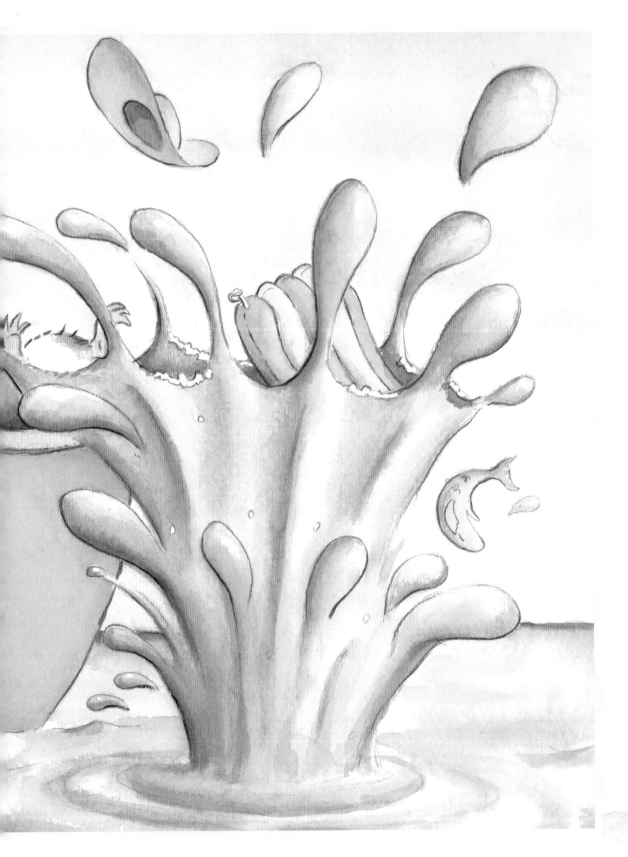

**wet guinea pigs.**

4-1=3

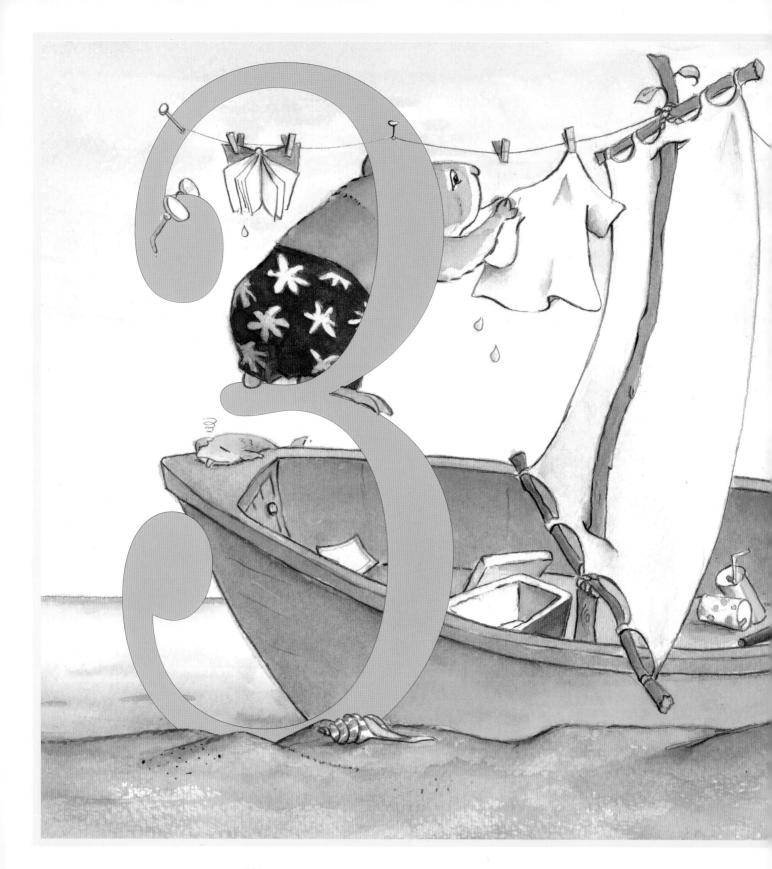

Three wet guinea pigs

**minus one greedy guinea pig**

leaves two

**thirsty guinea pigs.**

3-1=2

Two thirsty guinea pigs

minus one sleepy guinea pig

**= 1**

leaves just one guinea pig.

**And one...**

2-1=1

can be fun.